The Scarecrow and the Spider

Written and illustrated by

Todd Aaron Smith

Text & illustrations © 2005 by Todd Aaron Smith

Published in Nashville, Tennessee, by Tommy Nelson®, a Division of Thomas Nelson, Inc.

Tommy Nelson® books may be purchased in bulk for educational, business, fundraising, or sales promotion use. For information, please e-mail SpecialMarkets@ThomasNelson.com.

Library of Congress Cataloging-in-Publication Data

Smith, Todd Aaron.
  The scarecrow and the spider / written and illustrated by Todd Aaron Smith.
        p. cm.
  Summary: Benny, a lonely scarecrow, befriends a spider who explains that God is always watching over both of them.
   ISBN 1-4003-0550-0 (hardcover)
  [1. Scarecrows—Fiction. 2. Spiders—Fiction. 3. Christian life—Fiction.]   I. Title.
   PZ7.S6596Sca 2005
   [E]—dc22
                                                          2005001773

Printed in China
06 07 08 LEO 5 4 3 2

Para mi familia Mexicana
    …los quiero mucho.

—Todd

Visit Benny the Scarecrow on the Web at
www.toddaaronsmith.com

Benny the Scarecrow went for a stroll in the crisp, autumn breeze. As he reached a nearby pond, he saw that many birds and frogs were standing in and around the water. Maybe this would be his chance to make some new friends!

Benny smiled and waved his arms as he jumped out of the cornfield. "Hello, everyone!" he bellowed in his friendliest, loudest voice.

Suddenly there was complete panic at the pond! The birds and frogs all began jumping around, trying to get away.

The birds quickly flew over the trees, and the frogs all dove into the water! Benny was alone again.

Everything became very quiet. He peered sadly into the water, trying to find one of the frogs that had jumped into the pond. That's when he saw something startling. There was a frightening face looking back at him!

"Yikes!" Benny yelled, losing his balance and falling backward on the grass. He had never really seen what he looked like before. *No wonder everyone is scared of me,* he thought. His own reflection had scared even himself!

"That's why everyone is afraid of me," Benny said to himself as he lay in the grass, looking toward the sky. "Why was I made to be so different?"

Benny stood and walked along the bank of the pond. He passed by some reeds sticking up, and he noticed something very special. There, between the reeds, was a beautiful spider web.

"Wow!" Benny gasped as he admired the
spider's hard work. He was amazed that the tiny
spider had made such a beautiful home. Then Benny
saw something else. . . . A bird swooped down out of
the sky. The little spider dropped from her web to the
ground, while the bird circled around and quickly
headed straight for the spider!

Soon the bird was on the ground and moving closer! Benny knew that the bird would soon make a meal out of the little spider!

"Oh, NO! What can I do?" Benny sighed helplessly.

He looked around. There was no one else to help! Benny knew if he didn't do something right away, nobody would! But what *could* he do?

Hmm, the scarecrow thought. There was just one thing he could do. It was the thing that he could do better than anyone else. He realized he had been created for just one purpose.

Just as the bird was about to pounce on the helpless little spider, Benny jumped out from behind the reeds and yelled,

"Boo!"

The bird jumped and squawked. It took one look at the scarecrow and, in terror, flew away with lightning speed!

Benny fell to the ground to find the spider. He carefully picked her up, and she crawled into the palm of his hand.

Everything was quiet again. But, this time, Benny was not alone. They were together now . . . the scarecrow and the spider.

The spider danced around excitedly in Benny's hand. "Oh, I knew God was watching out for me!" she shouted with relief.

Benny tilted his head. "What do you mean?" he asked.

"God is always watching and taking care of me!" exclaimed the spider.

Benny looked to the ground. "I wish I had a friend like that."

"Oh, you do!" answered the spider. "God is always with us! Everywhere you go and in everything you do, God is there— even when you feel all alone!"

"That is the greatest thing I have ever heard," said Benny as he gently lifted the spider up to her web.

The two new friends talked for a long time, thankful to have found each other.

"You know, I've always wanted to find another friend too," the spider finally said. "But I've always seemed to scare people away."

"Me too." Benny smiled at the tiny spider.

Suddenly there was a rustling sound in the cornfield. "Someone's coming!" the spider exclaimed.

Benny glanced around. Then, seeing nowhere to hide, he fell limp to the ground.

"Look at that old scarecrow!" one of three boys yelled.

"Hey! I wonder if it'll float!" yelled another.

"Let's throw it in the pond!" laughed the third.

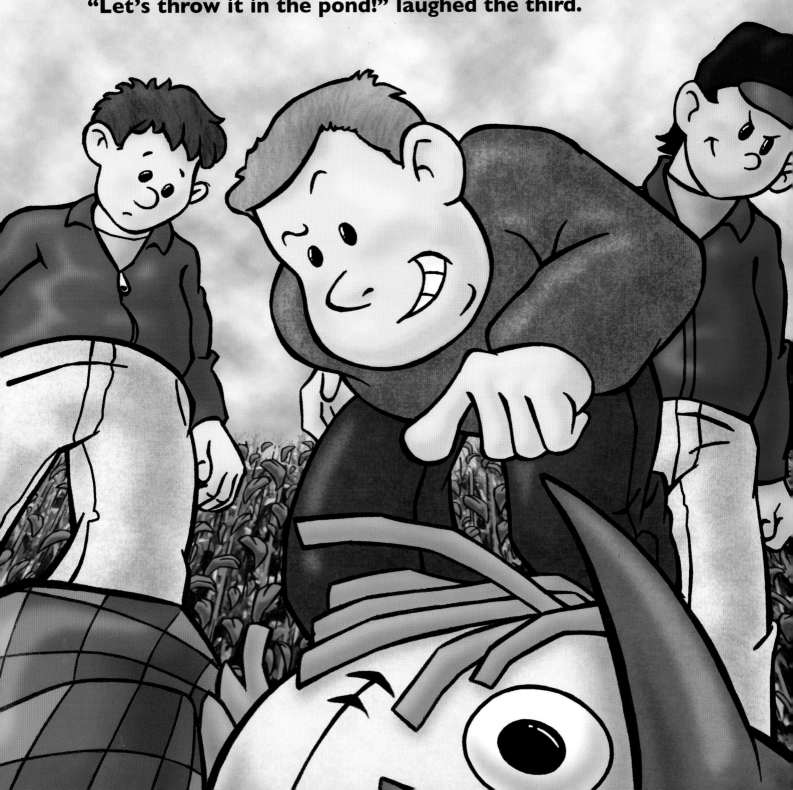

The boys picked up Benny and began swinging the motionless straw man back and forth.

"Ready? One . . . two . . . "

To help her new friend, the spider ran out of Benny's sleeve and onto the hand of one of the boys.

"AIIIEEEE!!" the boy yelped, dropping Benny's arms.

"Get it off! GET IT OFF!!"

The other boys dropped the scarecrow and circled
around the shrieking boy.

"Forget about that old scarecrow!" shouted the boy.
"It has spiders!"

"Ick! . . . Yucko!" Benny heard the boys yell as they ran
into the distance.

When the boys' voices faded, Benny lifted his head. "I guess that's why God made friends," he said. "Not just to share things, but to watch out for each other too."

"That makes sense," the spider replied. "That must be one of the ways that God takes care of us . . . by giving us friends."

That evening the scarecrow and the spider said goodbye, and Benny went back to his post in the field. A smile crossed the scarecrow's face as he thought about how he had never really been alone in the first place.

He looked toward the sky and was comforted by the spider's words: "God is there—even when you feel all alone."

That night, the scarecrow, knowing that God would
never leave him, said a prayer . . .
then drifted off to sleep.